FISH OUT
OF WATER

FISH OUT OF WATER

Joanne Levy

orca currents

ORCA BOOK PUBLISHERS

Published in Canada and the United States in 2020 by Orca Book Publishers.
orcabook.com

Library and Archives Canada Cataloguing in Publication
Title: Fish out of water / Joanne Levy.
Names: Levy, Joanne, author.
Series: Orca currents.
Description: Series statement: Orca currents
Identifiers: Canadiana (print) 20200175955 | Canadiana (ebook) 20200175963 |
ISBN 9781459826595 (softcover) | ISBN 9781459826601 (PDF) |
ISBN 9781459826618 (EPUB)
Classification: LCC PS8623.E9592 F58 2020 | DDC jc813/.6—dc23

Library of Congress Control Number: 2020930592

Summary: In this high-interest accessible novel for middle readers,
a twelve-year-old boy is frustrated that he's not able to
do the things he loves because they're too "girly."

Orca Book Publishers is committed to reducing the consumption of
nonrenewable resources in the making of our books. We make
every effort to use materials that support a sustainable future.

Orca Book Publishers gratefully acknowledges the support for its publishing
programs provided by the following agencies: the Government of Canada,
the Canada Council for the Arts and the Province of British Columbia
through the BC Arts Council and the Book Publishing Tax Credit.

Edited by Tanya Trafford
Design by Ella Collier
Cover artwork by Gettyimages/Francesco Carta fotografo
Author photo by Tania Garshowitz

Printed and bound in Canada.

23 22 21 20 • 1 2 3 4

For Travis, my friend

in crafting (and alpacas!).

Chapter One

"Let's go for ice cream."

My five favorite words in the entire world.

I turned away from the TV, which I wasn't really watching anyway, and looked up at my grandmother. She had been cleaning the kitchen after lunch but was now standing in the doorway, smiling. Her purse was over her shoulder, and her keys were in her hand. Ready to go.

"Yes, please, Bubby!" I jumped up off the couch. I was thankful for ice cream, but maybe even more for something to do.

Every Sunday I went to my grandparents' condo for a visit. It was pretty boring most of the time. I love them and all, but we never do anything.

They don't like the kind of movies I like. They don't want to go anywhere. And I hate watching sports, which seems to be the only thing my grandfather ever has on the TV. I guess my dad liked sports when he was alive. My zaida assumes that as a boy and his grandson, I do too. Out of respect, I watch when I visit. He seems to like it when we watch together. Most of the time, I just tune out.

Zaida was sitting in his big brown lounger, leaning way forward, very interested in the baseball game on the big screen. He obviously hadn't even heard the magic words.

"Zaida?" I barked to get his attention. "Come on. We're going for ice cream!"

Bubby shook her head. "He won't want to come."

Zaida glanced away from the TV to look at me. "You sure you don't want to stay here and watch the game? It's a nail-biter!"

"I'll be back later," I said. "You can catch me up." I didn't want to hurt his feelings.

"Suit yourself." He shrugged. "Bring home some chocolate mint?"

"Sure," Bubby said, jingling her keys. "Come on, Fishel. I need to stop at the yarn store too."

When we got to the front door, I worked my feet into my sneakers and followed her out.

We got into the elevator to ride down the eleven floors and then two more to the parking garage. "Do you need something special from the yarn store?" I asked. Because she always seemed to have lots of yarn at home.

"Yes." She sighed. "More sock yarn. One of my friends asked me to make a pair for her granddaughter's tenth birthday. On top of all the ones I've promised everyone else."

My grandmother was famous for her socks. She knitted them from special yarn and each pair was one of a kind. Well, two of a kind, I guess.

Each year at Hanukkah, I got three pairs that she had knitted just for me. Each set had a different pattern but was always made in my favorite colors—purple, pink and green. She spent hours and hours making them, her knitting needles click-clacking. It was kind of amazing actually. Sometimes I watched her knit, the yarn looping over the needles. Over and over. Her hands moved so fast they were a blur. More and more of the sock appeared below her needles, and the ball of yarn got smaller and smaller. It was like watching magic happen.

Then she'd get weird about me staring and tell me to go bug my grandfather.

When I wore the socks she made for me, I felt special. Like she was sending love and hugging my feet. Sounds weird, I know, but it's not really.

I thought my grandmother loved knitting. But her sigh made me wonder if something was wrong. "How come you don't seem happy about making them?"

She gave me a small smile as we got to the car. "Oh, I am. I just wish I didn't have so many requests."

"People love your socks, Bubby."

"They do. Not a terrible problem to have. Thank goodness they last a long time too—otherwise I'd never sleep. I'd spend every hour knitting to replace them as they wore out!"

We drove around and around up the ramp of the parking garage to get out. It made my stomach roll, almost like the rides at the fair.

We were out in the sunshine before she spoke again. "So, Fishel, have you decided on your bar mitzvah project yet?"

Ugh. Wasn't it enough that my mom and

Rabbi Seigel kept asking me if I'd figured it out yet? Apparently not. Everyone needed to know.

"Not yet," I said. "There's so much to do to prepare for my bar mitzvah. It feels like a full-time job."

You have to learn to read a part of the Torah in Hebrew and help your family plan your party. You also have to do a mitzvah—good deeds—project. It's not like in school either, where they tell you what assignment to do. You have to pick your own charity project. Something you're interested in.

My best friend, Seth, had decided he was going to collect used hockey gear. Then he'd give it out to kids who couldn't afford new equipment. He had said I could do it with him and that it would be fun to work together.

There was just one problem. I didn't like hockey. Or any sports. I didn't like watching them or playing them. The point of the project was to give of yourself to your community. Something meaningful.

Smelly old hockey equipment didn't feel all that

meaningful to me. Doing Seth's project with him would be my backup plan. One I hoped I wouldn't need.

But time was running out. All the other kids had picked their projects already. The rabbi had said I only had until our next class to decide.

"You'll think of something," Bubby said. "Maybe you could help serve at a soup kitchen or collect for a food bank."

"I guess," I said. Both of those things were important. But did I want to do either of them? Did I have something special to give to a soup kitchen or food bank? Not really.

Bubby turned on the radio and hummed along to the music as she drove. I looked out the window, thinking.

"Will you grab a basket, please?" Bubby said when we got inside the yarn store.

I was amazed at all the different kinds of yarn on the shelves lining the walls. So many colors! So many types! Thin, thick, fuzzy, soft, scratchy—how did a person decide?

My grandmother knew exactly what she needed. She walked straight over to the section marked *Sock Yarn.*

Of course.

She began tossing balls of yarn into my basket, muttering. "Two pairs for Fern. One for Silvia. Oh, and three for Frank's grandkids."

By the time she was done, the basket was nearly overflowing with yarn, in almost every color— black, red, brown, dark green, navy blue and even multicolored.

"Whoa!" I said. "How many pairs do you have to make?"

"Don't ask," she said as the clerk rang up the bill. The very big bill. I wondered if her friends paid her for the yarn.

When I asked her if they did, she smiled and shook her head. "My socks are a labor of love—I love making them for people, and they love receiving them. It feels good to give them away."

"Maybe I could help you," I said.

Bubby laughed. "Oh, Fishel. If only." She gave me a side hug.

As she handed the clerk her credit card, I got an idea.

A great idea. A really amazing, perfect, super-special idea.

BAM. Just like that, standing in the middle of the yarn store, I'd come up with my mitzvah project.

Chapter Two

I love ice cream, but I barely tasted my caramel cone. My brain was too busy whirling with ideas. I couldn't wait to get back to the condo and start on my plan.

When we got there, and after we had taken Zaida his ice cream, I followed Bubby to her yarn room. It's also my bedroom when I sleep over.

"Fishel, what's with you?" said Bubby. "Why are you so...bouncy?"

"I'm excited!" I grinned at her. "I need you to teach me how to knit."

She frowned. "What do you mean?"

"I want to learn how to knit. Will you teach me?"

"Fishel," she said sternly, shaking her head, "knitting isn't for boys."

My heart sunk. "What do you mean? Why is it just for girls?"

Bubby clucked her tongue and turned her back to me. She began to stack the new yarn on her shelves. "It just is. Why don't you go watch the game with your zaida?"

"Because I don't want to." I sat on the bed. "I want to learn how to make socks." I had been about to tell her my idea for my mitzvah project. Now I wasn't sure I wanted to.

What did being a boy or a girl have to do with knitting? Knitting was something you did with your hands. I had two hands just like any girl. It didn't make any sense.

My bubby leaned over and grabbed my chin, giving it a squeeze. She smiled at me. "Fishel, you're so kind, wanting to help me. But you should be playing outside and climbing trees, not knitting like an old lady."

Like an old lady? Now knitting wasn't just a *girl* thing but an *old lady* thing? There had been plenty of people at the yarn store. Not all of them were old. Although, as I thought about it, they were all women. Why? I wore knitted socks, so why couldn't I make them too?

I almost dropped the subject, but something told me to keep going. I cleared my throat and said, "Bubby, what if I really want to knit? Even though I'm a boy?"

She frowned again. "Wouldn't you like to learn woodworking? Or I saw a poster at the community center for beginner karate. How about something like that?"

Woodworking? Karate? Was she even listening to me? Did she know me at all?

"No," I said, crossing my arms. "I don't want to do anything like that. I want to knit."

"Fishel," she said, using that disappointed-parent tone.

My eyes started to sting. Why was it such a big deal?

The door buzzer sounded.

"Your mother is here," said Bubby. She sounded relieved. She gave me a quick kiss on the forehead. "Go say goodbye to your zaida. We'll see you next week."

And as quickly as I had found an idea for my project, it was gone just as fast.

"How was your visit?" Mom asked when I climbed in the back seat.

I was still sort of mad at my bubby, but when I saw my little sister, strapped into her car seat, smiling and reaching out for me, I felt a bit better. "Hi, Norah,"

I said, grabbing her chubby little hand. "How are you, cutie?"

Bubby and Zaida aren't Norah's grandparents. They're my dad's parents. He died when I was five. Three years ago Mom married Darren. Then they had Norah. I'd always wanted a sister, and now I've got one. Darren's okay too.

Norah gurgled and blew a wet raspberry at me. I blew one back. She giggled. She's not much fun to play with yet, but she thinks I'm hilarious.

"Fish?" Darren said, looking in the mirror at me. "Your mom asked you a question."

"Oh. Sorry," I said. "It was fine."

Mom turned around in her seat to look at me straight on. "Just fine?" She stared at me, waiting for an answer. I wondered if I should tell her my plan.

"Do you know how to knit?" I asked instead.

She tilted her head. "No," she said. "But I always wished I'd learned."

"Bubby could teach you," I said.

"Yes, she knits so beautifully." Mom smiled. "She has offered to teach me a few times over the years, but who has the time?"

So my grandmother was willing to teach my mom. But not me. I felt myself getting mad again. I looked out the window. It didn't seem fair.

"Maybe one day you'll learn to knit," Mom said.

Yes! I turned, excited to tell her about my plan.

She was looking at Norah in her car seat.

She'd been talking to my sister.

I let out a big sigh.

"What's wrong, Fish?" Mom asked.

"Nothing. Never mind." I turned back toward the window.

"Oh, I almost forgot," she said. "While you were with your bubby and zaida, we went down to the JCC."

"Great," I said. Why was she even telling me this? Why would I care that she went to the Jewish Community Center?

"We signed up for Mommy and Me gymnastics."

"What?" I frowned. "I'm a little too old to go to gymnastics with you."

My mom laughed. "Not for you and me, Fish. For Norah and me."

I chuckled. "Oh, right. That's great."

"Aaaaaand," she said, smiling like something cool was coming.

"And?" I asked. The way she was looking at me made me scared that what she thought was cool wasn't. I was suddenly filled with dread.

"I signed you up for water polo."

"*Water polo?*"

She nodded. Excitedly. Like water polo was cool.

"Why would you sign me up for water polo?"

"It's a great sport," said Darren, catching my eye in the mirror again. "I played it all through high school and college. It'll build strength and character."

Strength and character? Ugh. Darren was nice and all, but *seriously*?

"What if I don't want to do water polo?"

Mom blinked at me, confused. "Oh, I thought you would be excited about it. It's the only thing offered at the same time as the Mommy and Me class. The three of us can go down there together."

I sighed.

"Unless you want to do Zumba," she added with a wink.

"Zumba?" I asked. "Isn't that the dance class you do sometimes?" I actually really like dancing. *Dancing with the Stars* is my favorite show.

"It's a workout class," Mom said, laughing. "But this one's for seniors. Most of them probably come over from the retirement home next door. I was only kidding, Fish. I don't think you want to do Zumba with a bunch of old people."

"Oh."

"Anyway, we start this Wednesday after school."

"I don't know," I said. "I have bar mitzvah lessons, plus homework, and I still have to figure out my charity project." I couldn't believe I was bringing *that* up, but I was desperate. I really did not want to do water polo.

"It's just one hour a week," Mom said.

"You'll love it," Darren added.

I seriously doubted it. But what could I do?

"Fine," I said. "I just have one question."

"What's that?" Mom asked, smiling.

I shrugged. "What on earth *is* water polo?"

Chapter Three

"What's the problem?" Seth asked the next morning. "Water polo sounds like fun!" We were on the school bus, sitting in our regular seat—third from the back on the left. It was only the second week of school, but we'd picked our spot on the very first day. Our friends Amir and Steven sat in the seat in front of us.

"Not to me," I said. "I'd rather do Zumba."

Seth's face scrunched up. "What's Zumba? Like kickboxing or something?"

"No. It's like dancing."

"Dancing?"

I shrugged. "Never mind." Seth didn't get dancing. He'd never even watched *DWTS*.

"You're weird, bro," Seth said. He didn't mean it though. At least, not in a bad way. We'd been best friends for a long time.

"Yeah, well, you're weird for playing hockey and getting your teeth knocked out!" I didn't mean that in a bad way either. I didn't really get why Seth loved hockey so much. I guess in the same way he didn't get why I loved dancing.

Seth smiled, showing off the big gap in his mouth where a tooth used to be. He didn't actually lose the tooth from hockey. He was just late getting all his grown-up teeth. Could happen though.

"Speaking of hockey," he said, "you should see what we collected at the rink on Saturday. So. Much.

Stuff. I'm going to crush my mitzvah project!"

"That's great," I said. "But I'm not sure the point is to win."

"It is if a ton of kids get equipment." He put up his hand for a high five. "Winning!"

I left him hanging, rolling my eyes instead of high-fiving him back.

"Bro!" he yelled. When I finally gave in and slapped his palm with mine, he nodded. "That's what I'm talking about."

I rolled my eyes again. "You're a dork."

He grinned at me. "So. You going to do the project with me or what?"

I took a breath, not sure how to answer yet.

"Because Coach said we have room for one more kid to help. I told him you were going to do it. So, you know, you sort of have to."

"Seriously, Seth?" I laughed.

My best friend shrugged. "Well, you don't *have* to. But don't you *want* to?"

I thought about the idea I'd come up with at the yarn store. Not much chance of doing that without my grandmother's help. But did I want to do the sports thing? If I did, I'd be stuck with it as my mitzvah project for the next several months.

Ugh. But what choice did I have?

The bus pulled to a stop in the school's parking lot. The front doors opened.

"*Maybe* I'll do it with you," I said.

Seth put his hand up for another high five, so I quickly added, "But maybe not. I'm still figuring it out. I'll let you know when we go to our bar mitzvah class on Thursday. I have to tell the rabbi what I'm doing then anyway."

I hoped to come up with something else by then. Almost anything else.

I was still thinking about it as I followed Seth into the school.

Then I saw it. A sign on the wall.

Knitting Club

Library at lunchtime

Beginners welcome!

I turned to Seth. "Tell your coach he can find someone else."

Seth glanced at the poster. Then he looked at me. "Seriously? What's going on here, Fishel?"

"I can't tell you yet. But it'll be really cool," I said, so excited I could barely keep it in. "Trust me."

Seth muttered, "You're acting really weird, dude."

Before I could respond, the bell rang. We hurried to class.

By lunchtime I was getting pretty nervous. So nervous that I kept dropping my books.

"Come on, Fish," Seth said, slamming his locker closed. "There's going to be a huge line in the caf!"

"Just go ahead," I said. "I'm not eating with you today."

"What do you mean?"

I looked at him. "I'm going to the knitting club."

"*What?*"

I guess he had already forgotten the sign we'd seen earlier.

"I'm going to learn to knit," I said.

He snorted. "No, you're not." He grabbed my sleeve. "Come on, dork. Steve and Amir are probably already waiting for us."

I yanked my arm back and bent down to get my lunch out of my backpack. "I mean it. I'm going to Knitting Club."

"With the *girls*?" Seth asked.

I looked up at him. "So? What if there are girls?"

He crossed his arms. "You want to do something *girly*?"

I stood up and crossed my arms. "What does that even mean?"

He rolled his eyes. "Girly? You know, stuff that girls do."

"What's your problem?" I asked, my face growing hot.

"What's your problem, Fish?" said Seth, frowning. "Do you want to be a girl?"

Why would he even ask that? Just because I wanted to learn how to knit? "No," I replied. "But—"

"So why do you want to act like one?" He looked at me like I had a disease or something.

"I'm not acting like anything!" I said, furious now. "Why do you want to act like a jerk, Seth?" The words were out of my mouth before I could stop them.

He looked shocked. "Whatev, bro," he said finally. "Or should I say, *sis*. I'd rather be a jerk than a *girl*."

And then he was gone, marching down the hall away from me.

I stood there, confused. What had just happened? What had made my best friend so mad? All I wanted to do was learn how to make socks.

Why would learning to knit make me a girl?

And what was wrong with being a girl anyway?

Chapter Four

I almost didn't go. Seth's words had upset me so much that I started to wonder if going was even worth it. But the more I thought about it, the madder I got. Why was he so mean? I never told him he shouldn't play hockey. Who was he to tell me what *I* couldn't do?

I slammed my locker closed and made my way to the library. When I got inside, it was quiet. Maybe no one had come? But then I saw the whiteboard by the door. Knitting Club was being held in the group study room. I headed through the stacks of books toward the back of the library.

When I was almost there, I heard voices. I stopped to listen.

"Welcome, girls!" I recognized Ms. Harper's voice. I'd never had her as a teacher, but she seemed nice. She was younger than my mom and wore fancy dresses with cool designs on them. Stuff like math formulas or science things.

"I hope you're all excited to get started!"

There were a few voices, but I couldn't tell how many people were in there. It wasn't a big room—probably eight seats around the big rectangular table. I was scared to take a peek.

Then it hit me. Ms. Harper had said, "Welcome, *girls*." Maybe this was a girls-only club. It hadn't said so on the poster, but maybe everyone was right. Maybe knitting really *was* for girls. Was I even allowed to be here? Maybe boys weren't allowed, and everyone—except me—knew it.

Feeling stupid, I turned to leave. My lunch bag fell out of my hand. I squatted down to pick it up.

"Hello?"

Busted.

"Fishel, right?" I stood up and turned around. Ms. Harper was in the study room doorway, smiling. Today's dress was black with stars on it. It reminded me of when I'd gone camping with Seth and his family. At night the sky had been so clear, we could see every single star.

I recognized the Big Dipper by Ms. Harper's right shoulder.

"Oh, hi," I said, feeling my face heat up again.

"Are you here for Knitting Club?"

I almost said no. But she was smiling, and she looked…hopeful?

"If…you know…um…if that's okay," is what I did say.

"Great!" she said and stood back, waving me into the room. "Grab a seat. We're just getting started."

I stepped inside and looked around. Four girls sat at the table—Ginny Freeman, Gail Wu, Mandy López, and a girl I didn't know. She was seated by herself way at the end of the table. Ginny and Gail might as well be twins, because they did everything together.

Sort of like how they were both staring at me now. I put my lunch on the table and sat down next to Mandy.

"Hey," I said to her, giving her a big smile.

She frowned. "Hi." She was looking at me hard. I tried not to fidget in my seat, but all those girls staring at me made me feel weird.

"So," Ms. Harper said. "For this first meeting, we'll get to know each other a little and then go over the basics. Why don't you get out your lunches? I'll talk while you eat."

There were a few minutes of crinkling and shuffling sounds. I opened my bento box—hummus, carrots, celery, cheese and a couple of Mom's homemade chocolate-chunk cookies. I offered one to Mandy, but she shook her head.

Ms. Harper continued. "We'll meet here every Monday. And I'll probably be here most lunch periods on the other days too. So if you want to get some help between meetings, or if you just want to hang out and knit, you're more than welcome."

"Cool," Gail said. "It's way better in here than in the noisy cafeteria."

Speaking of the cafeteria, I wondered what Seth was telling our friends about where I was right now.

"Let's start with introductions," Ms. Harper said. "Your name, if you've done any knitting before and what you'd like to accomplish here. Mandy? Why don't you start?"

Mandy introduced herself, but I didn't hear the rest of her speech. I was too focused on what *I* was going to say. My name was easy enough. Also that I'd never knitted anything. But what did I want to accomplish? My mitzvah project was still a secret for now, while I was figuring it out. I wasn't ready to share it yet.

When it was my turn, I cleared my throat. "I'm Fishel—Fish—Rosner. I've never done any knitting before, but I'd like to learn how to make socks. Like the ones I'm wearing."

Ms. Harper's eyebrows went up. "Oh, can we see?"

I stood up, slipped off my left shoe, kicked my leg up and rested it on the back of my chair. I pulled up my pant leg so everyone could see the green, pink and purple stripes.

"Oh, those are beautiful!" Ms. Harper said, leaning forward. "Did someone make those for you?"

I nodded and sat down, pushing my foot back into my shoe. "My grandmother."

"Well, aren't you lucky?"

I was relieved she didn't ask me why my bubby wasn't teaching me to knit. What would I have said?

She moved on to Ginny and Gail, who wanted to work together to make sweaters for their dogs. The last girl, whose name was Barbie Hendriks, said she wanted to learn to knit because her aunt was having a baby. She wanted to make a baby blanket as a shower gift.

"These are all great reasons to want to learn to knit," Ms. Harper said. "It's also a wonderful stress reliever. Some say it's meditative, which means it helps you calm your mind and focus. I agree. Making things with your hands is rewarding in itself too. The results of your efforts are right in front of you. And, of course, it's nice to be able to make gifts for people." She smiled at Gail and Ginny. "And dogs."

Gail and Ginny grinned.

"I have been knitting since I was about your age," Ms. Harper continued. "And I love to teach! So I'm really looking forward to us knitting and learning together.

"Today we're going to practice casting on. Next week we'll start with some basic stitches."

She picked up a stack of papers from the table in front of her and counted out five sheets. She passed them to Ginny to hand around. "These are some of the stitches and projects we'll be doing over the next few weeks. You're welcome to bring your own supplies, of course, but you may want to try a few of mine for a few weeks until you figure out what is most comfortable." She lifted a large wicker basket onto the table. It was filled with balls of yarn and long silver needles of different sizes.

I glanced down at my sheet. It was going to take weeks before I'd have...a dishcloth? *We were going to be making dishcloths?* That was not what I was expecting.

I put up my hand.

"Yes, Fishel?" Ms. Harper said as she handed me a giant pair of needles.

"I...um...I don't really want to make a dishcloth.

I was hoping to make socks." Maybe she needed a reminder of why I was there.

Ms. Harper chuckled. "No one wants to make dishcloths," she said. "But it's a great way to learn the basics. And you'll have something at the end that you can take home."

"But...I want to take home *socks*," I said. "We already have dishcloths."

"So do we," Ginny said as she exchanged a look with Gail, who was nodding.

Ms. Harper smiled. "I understand. But first you have to learn the basics. Socks, especially ones like the beautiful pair you're wearing, aren't a beginner project. I'm sure your grandmother had to practice a lot before she was able to perfect them."

I'd never thought about it. As far back as I could remember, Bubby had knitted. I didn't know if she had ever taken lessons. It had always seemed like she simply knew how to do everything. She just did it. But it made sense that she would have had a lot of practice. I had assumed it was easy to knit. Like tying your shoes—you learned it and then you did it for the rest of your life without even thinking about it.

We spent the rest of the lunch period trying to get yarn onto our needles. It was way harder than it looked and so slow.

When my bubby knitted, she clicked and clacked her needles so fast, it was a blur. She almost never even had to look at what she was doing.

But every loop of yarn was a challenge for me. I had to hold the needles, wrap the yarn, and then poke it up and over just the right way. Ugh. It was going to take forever. To make a dishcloth I didn't want.

Ms. Harper asked what color of yarn we wanted to use for our dishcloths. I told her whatever color she picked for me was fine. The truth was, I didn't really care.

In fact, I probably wasn't going to come back to Knitting Club. What was the point? There was no way I was going to be good enough in time to do what I wanted for my bar mitzvah project.

The five-minute bell rang, and we all got up to leave.

"Fishel?" Ms. Harper said. "Stay behind for a second?"

Uh-oh.

Chapter Five

Stay behind for a second.

My stomach lurched. Was I in trouble?

Ms. Harper looked at me kindly and said, "Fishel, you're going to come back next week, aren't you?"

How did she know what was in my head? I shrugged. "Maybe knitting isn't for me."

She tilted her head. "Why do you say that?"

"I don't know."

"Sit back down for a second." She pointed at my chair. "Don't worry about being late," she added before I could protest. "I'll give you a pass for next period."

I dropped back into my chair. She sat in the one beside me.

"Talk to me, Fish. I promise, whatever it is, you're safe telling me."

I focused my eyes down at the project sheet.

"Fishel?"

"It's hard," I said after a moment.

"Many things worth doing are hard," she said.

"I guess."

"Is that the only thing that's bothering you, Fish?"

I sighed. "People don't get it. That maybe a boy wants to knit."

"Ah," she said, leaning back. "Well, *I* get it. I get it maybe as well as anyone."

How could she? I looked up at her.

She nodded. "I'm a math and physics nerd. I was one of only a few women in my classes at university.

Actually, in some classes I was the only woman. A lot of people told me I'd never succeed. So you know what I did?"

"Became a teacher?"

"Eventually," she said. "But only after I told all those people to stuff it, and I studied everything I wanted to. I love math. I don't care if it's something women don't normally do. It's my life, and I'm not going to let anyone stand in the way of me following my passions."

Ms. Harper seemed so sure of herself. I couldn't imagine anyone telling her she couldn't do something.

She smiled. "Do you understand what I'm saying?"

"I think so," I said. I might have sounded a bit unsure, but the truth was, I *totally* understood. My family had said basically the same thing to me. Somehow she knew it. Maybe math wasn't her only superpower.

"I'm sorry if you're feeling pressure to do what other people expect. I think that's even more reason for you to stay in Knitting Club though. Show them they're wrong. Be your own person and trust that you know what's best for you."

I nodded. "Okay."

"Good." She smiled widely, like she'd just solved all my problems.

Except that she hadn't.

"I mean, yeah," I said. "That's part of it. But also... you know, the socks. I really want to make socks."

Ms. Harper sighed. "I know you do, Fish, but it will take a lot of practice before you will be ready to do such a complicated project. You'd be setting yourself up to fail, I'm afraid."

I thought about that stinky hockey equipment I'd have to collect. "Can I try though, Ms. Harper? Please?"

She laughed. "You're very determined, aren't you?"

I nodded.

"Why is making socks so important to you, Fish?"

I shook my head. "No reason." What was the point of telling her my big idea? It was going to be a total bust anyway.

Her eyebrows went up. She knew there was more to the story.

I realized I had nothing to lose. I told her about my mitzvah project plan. Her reaction was *not* what I was expecting.

"That's not 'no reason'!" she exclaimed. Her eyes were wide. She looked really excited. She put her hands on my shoulders. "That's a *great* reason, Fish!" She was so nice. And she got it. She got *me*.

"Thanks," I said. "But there's no way I can do it now if it's going to take forever to learn."

"Well, that *is* probably true. If you weren't an absolute beginner, it might be possible."

"Yeah, I know," I said. I was super bummed.

Ms. Harper was quiet for a few moments. Finally she said, "How about this: You work on learning the basics with the group. And then, if you still want to, you can come in for extra lunch periods so you and I can work on a pair of socks together as a side project."

"Really?" I asked, suddenly excited again.

"Sure," she said. She grabbed a late slip out of her bag, scribbled on it and handed it to me. "Then, once you get good at it, you can make all the socks you want. But I'll only agree to it if you promise to work hard on learning the basics on our regular club day."

"I will. I promise," I said, stuffing the paper into my pocket.

"All right then." She stood up and waved toward the door. "You'd better get to class. I'll see you next week, Fish."

I opened my mouth. I was about to ask if I could come the next day to get started.

She shook her head. "I know what you're going to say, and no. We will start next week—I don't want you jumping ahead of the other kids."

"Okay," I said with a grin—she really did get me. I grabbed my backpack and started to leave.

"Fish?" she said as I got to the doorway.

I looked over my shoulder.

"I'm really proud of you."

"Thank you," I said, feeling a bit weird. "I like your dress," I added. Then I jogged out of the library.

She was proud of me.

It felt nice. But I couldn't help wishing that others were too.

Because I was late for my next class and it had already started, it wasn't until after school that I realized Seth was still upset with me.

It was stupid—he had been mean to me. I was the one who should be upset. I mean, I was. And yeah, I had called him a jerk. But I still planned to sit with him on the school bus home. We'd make up and be best friends again.

He had other ideas though.

When I got onto the bus, I saw right away that he was still being a jerk.

Steven, Amir and Seth were all squashed together on one seat. Our seat. There was no room left for me.

Steven and Amir's regular seat in front of ours was empty. But I could tell by the way they were all glaring at me that they didn't want me near them. I didn't want to sit near them either.

I didn't need three kids being mean to me. What had Seth told the others? And why? I still didn't understand why he was so mad.

I turned toward Karla, the bus driver. "Can I sit up here?"

The front seat right behind the door was usually empty. Sometimes her son sat there if he had a day off from day care. But today only a giant purse was in the seat.

Karla frowned. "Of course you can," she said. "But is everything okay, Fish?" She knew I always sat with Seth.

No. Nothing was okay. But what could she do? She couldn't make my friends stop being jerks.

"Yep," I said. "I just thought it would be nice to sit up front for a change. Take in the scenery, you know?"

I gave her a big smile, like everything was totally normal.

She gave me a weird look but didn't say anything else.

Chapter Six

"Excited for your first water-polo lesson?" Mom asked as she pulled the car out of our driveway. She'd picked me up at school on Wednesday, which had saved me from having to sit alone at the front of the bus again.

"Sure," I said. Which was code for "not even a little." Not that she understood code. Obviously.

I still couldn't believe they were making me go. But it was a done deal. Darren worked late on Wednesdays, and Mom said I couldn't stay home alone. I tried to tell her I was mature enough and would just sit at the kitchen table and do my homework I wouldn't turn on the stove, play with matches or answer the door to any strangers.

She was having none of it. She reminded me that we did things as a family. Her tone made me think that arguing wouldn't get me out of water polo but might get me grounded. So I didn't bother.

Off we went to the JCC.

"Fishel?" Mom looked at me in the rearview mirror when we were almost there. "You'll have a good time. You liked swimming lessons, didn't you?"

Didn't she realize I'd only gone to swimming lessons so I could learn how not to drown? Water polo (I'd googled it) was basically soccer in the water. I was not a good swimmer, not even an okay soccer player, and I hated team sports. Water polo was pretty much my worst nightmare.

"Sure, Mom," I said.

"You'll enjoy yourself once you get into it and meet the other kids."

Beside me Norah blew a raspberry. Even *she* knew water polo was the worst.

I made her laugh with a silly face.

When we got to the JCC, I helped Norah out of her car seat and handed her and the diaper bag to Mom. I grabbed my backpack and followed them in. Slowly. To my doom.

"Oh come on, Fishel," Mom said. "Stop being so dramatic."

When we got inside, Mom pointed down the hall. "You remember the men's changerooms are down there? You can check in at the counter. We'll meet you in the lobby after. Have fun!"

My sister waved bye-bye at me over Mom's shoulder as they headed to their class. I waved back.

With a sigh, I started toward the changerooms. I heard music start. Fun music.

I was drawn to an open door down the hall. The music had a fast beat that made me want to move along with it. Then the singing began. It took me a few moments to realize the words were in another language. Whatever it was, I liked it.

"Hi there!"

A man was standing in the corner of the room by a stereo. He was wearing shorts, a JCC T-shirt and bright blue sneakers.

"Oh, hi."

"You here for seniors' Zumba?" he asked with a goofy smile.

I laughed. "No, I just noticed the music. I like it."

The man nodded. "Zumba music is really danceable—that's what makes it fun. Latin vibes."

"I should go," I said, pointing down the hall. "I have...water polo."

The guy snorted. "You don't look very happy about it."

"I'm not, to be honest."

He shrugged. "Well, this is a seniors' class, but I think you could keep up. If you want to join in, I mean."

"Really?"

"Fine by me, as long as you square it with the office. We start in"—he glanced up at the clock on the wall—"eight minutes."

"Okay," I said, my heart pounding with excitement. "I...I...might be back."

When I got out into the hall, I stopped in my tracks. Was I doing this? I looked toward the check-in desk. A bored-looking guy sat there, staring at his phone.

Could I do this?

I suddenly heard Ms. Harper's voice in my head. *I'm not going to let anyone stand in the way of me following my passions.*

Was Zumba my passion?

No way to know just yet. But one thing I did know for sure.

Water polo was not.

Chapter Seven

I ran down the hall toward the changerooms. I yanked off my jeans and pulled on my swimsuit, which was basically shorts. My T-shirt would have to do. I stuffed my feet back into my sneakers. I shoved my bag into a locker and sprinted to the Zumba room.

When I got there, I stopped in the doorway. It was full of...well...old people. There were four ladies, maybe about my grandmother's age. They all wore sweats in different bright colors. There were also three older men near the back of the room. Their outfits were less colorful. One guy was *really* old and was leaning on a walker. The other two stood next to him, talking.

I shouldn't have been surprised that they were all old. It *was* a seniors' class. But now that I was standing there, I felt weird. Too young. Very out of place. Like I didn't belong.

Would I have felt any better in water polo? No. Definitely not. At least in Zumba I wasn't going to drown. And I would get to dance.

I took a deep breath and stepped into the room.

"Hey, you're back!" the instructor said, smiling. "Come on in. I'm Richard."

All eyes were on me. If I was feeling out of place a minute ago, I *really* felt out of place now. Maybe in fifty years I'd fit in. "I'm Fish," I said, my voice squeaky.

"Fish?" one of the old men repeated. "Like gefilte fish?" Then he winked at me.

I laughed. My bubby sometimes called me Gefilte Fish, especially around the high holidays when she was making the fish patties for our special dinners. Fish patties might sound gross, but they are actually really good.

"It's short for Fishel," I said, suddenly feeling better for some reason.

"Fishel?" one of the ladies said. "You're Sandy Rosner's grandson, aren't you?"

I nodded.

"I'm Maggie Cohen," she said. "I met you at your bubby's birthday party last year, remember?"

I didn't, but I nodded anyway. "Nice to see you again," I said. Bubby always said to be extra polite to her friends.

"Come on over here, Fish," Richard said, waving me into the room. He introduced me to the rest of the people in the class. I forgot all their names almost immediately, except for Mrs. Cohen. But not a single one of them told me I shouldn't be there. They just smiled and said it was nice to meet me.

Richard turned on the music and took his spot at the front of the room.

"Why don't you come up here, Fish," he said, "since you're new. You'll be able to follow along. These *alter kockers* have been doing this forever. They probably do it in their sleep." I giggled. I had heard that Yiddish phrase before. It means "old fart." Sometimes Bubby called Zaida that when she thought he wouldn't hear her.

I made my way up to the front row. Richard turned and faced away from us, but the whole wall was a mirror, so we could see him. It felt weird to watch myself too.

But as Richard started calling out the dance steps to the music, it made sense. Seeing myself in the mirror made it easier to follow along with what Richard was doing.

Which I did. From one song to the next, I danced and danced, feeling the music and listening to Richard call out what to do next. I stopped feeling weird about all the other people in the room. I followed pretty well, but it didn't matter if I fumbled a step or two. I just kept on dancing with Richard and the old people. We were all smiling and laughing.

Fifty minutes passed so quickly, I almost couldn't believe the class was over. I was hot and sweaty. I had spent the whole time dancing, and I couldn't stop smiling. I couldn't remember when I had ever felt better. Even ice cream didn't make me feel as good.

Zumba was my new favorite thing.

"Great class, everyone!" Richard said, clapping. We all clapped too and gave him our thanks.

I turned to leave. I had to hurry to the changerooms

for a shower and then meet my mom and Norah. But Richard called my name.

I stopped and turned.

"So? How did you like the class?" he asked.

"I loved it!"

He smiled back. "I thought you might. You did great with the steps. Are you sure this was your first time?"

"Yep," I said, happy because I'd impressed him.

"Well, you wouldn't know it. And..." He looked around and leaned in close. "They liked having you here."

I frowned. "Really?"

He nodded. "Sure. You were obviously having a good time, and so they were too—it's infectious."

"I did have a good time. A really good time."

"So you'll come back?"

"I hope I can." I nodded. "This was way better than water polo."

Richard chuckled. "I hear you, kid."

"I'd better go," I said.

Richard gave me a fist bump. I raced to the changerooms.

I chickened out.

I had planned to tell Mom that I'd switched from water polo to Zumba. But I couldn't figure out how. Plus, what if she got mad? What if Darren was disappointed that I hadn't gone to water polo?

But my biggest worry? What if they wouldn't let me do it again next week?

When I got to the lobby, my hair was still wet. Mom assumed it was from the pool. It was easier to go along with that. When she asked how the class was, I said I'd had a good hour. Not technically a lie.

"How was gymnastics?" I asked as I buckled Norah into her seat.

She blew a raspberry.

I laughed. "That bad?"

Mom chuckled as she got behind the wheel. "It was great, actually. Norah had a good time, no matter what she tells you."

My sister smiled and blew me a kiss. I wondered if she would care that I hadn't gone to water polo.

Probably not.

Chapter Eight

Later that night we were all at the kitchen table, eating chicken stir-fry. Darren's favorite.

Mom, Darren and I had big bowls in front of us. We were eating with chopsticks. I wondered if the first knitting needles were made of chopsticks. That would make sense. I thought about googling it later.

Norah had her dinner—rice, chicken and vegetables—on her high-chair tray. She ate the pieces with her fingers.

"I knew you'd love water polo," Darren said.

Huh? I never said I'd loved water polo. But I wasn't going to argue. The quicker we changed the subject, the better. I was still worried about getting busted for taking Zumba instead. Now I was risking getting busted for lying about it too.

"I wish I didn't have this shoulder injury or I'd still play," Darren said with a frown. "Water polo is the perfect sport."

Perfectly *awful*, I thought. "This stir-fry is really good, Mom," I said.

Mom smiled. "Thanks, honey."

Darren took a bite and then pointed his chopstick at me. "Water polo's a great workout too."

Ugh. We were *still* talking about this? He was

staring at me, waiting for an answer. Even though he hadn't asked a question.

I thought about all the dancing and how sweaty I'd gotten in the Zumba class. "I got a great workout today." Which was totally true.

"Good for you, Fish," Mom said. "It's great to try new things."

"I enjoyed the new things I tried today." Another truth.

"Aaaaand," she said, a goofy look on her face, "you were a fish. In water!"

"Har, har," Darren said, rolling his eyes at the terrible joke.

"Fish!" Norah blurted, throwing a piece of chicken at Darren.

That we all laughed at.

Finally the subject changed to the Mommy and Me class. Mom went on and on about Norah's amazing gymnastic skills. It was funny because

Norah's basically a baby and can't do much of anything.

But still, Mom going on about it was a relief. It meant I was off the hook.

For now.

Chapter Nine

The next day was Thursday. Seth still wasn't talking to me. Neither were Steven and Amir. They kept glaring at me. I didn't know what Seth had told them. It wasn't good, obviously. Not that I wanted to talk to Seth yet anyway.

But Seth and I were going to have to make up eventually. His mom was picking us up after school to go to our bar mitzvah class. He couldn't be mean to me in his mom's car. Could he?

I spent lunch in the library, avoiding my friends. After I'd eaten I looked at a bunch of books about knitting for beginners.

I sort of knew how to cast on from our class. So I skipped ahead to study the step-by-step pictures of actual knitting. I took pictures with my brain, memorizing the steps.

It didn't look all that complicated though. I felt confident that with more practice I'd be pretty good at it.

So confident that I found a different book, called *Knit to Wear*. There was a family on the cover, all wearing knitted clothes—including socks that looked like the ones Bubby had made me. That's what really drew my attention.

I took the book back to my table. But when I opened it and flipped to the section about socks, my heart sank.

I'd thought Ms. Harper was exaggerating when she said socks were not a beginner project. I'd thought if I studied and worked hard, I'd be able to figure them out. Then I'd be able to do the mitzvah project.

Looking at the sock patterns, I couldn't make sense of any of the words—the patterns seemed to be written in code! Ms. Harper was right—I'd totally fail if I tried to make socks without lots of practice first.

I was doomed to collect stinky hockey equipment.

But only if I could make up with my best friend first.

Sigh.

Truth was, even though I was still mad at him, I missed him.

Riding the bus with Karla's purse was lonely.

I thought Seth would try to make up with me by the end of the day for sure. I even spent a few extra minutes at my locker in case he wanted to say he was sorry.

He was taking his time, chatting with people at his locker, his back to me. He was even talking to Mandy, which seemed weird. He'd never talked to her before.

Was he asking her about Knitting Club? I couldn't really hear what they were saying, but I was very curious.

Maybe better not to know, I thought. I got all my stuff and headed out to the school parking lot.

When I got outside, Seth's mom was already there. Her black minivan was in her regular spot. I pulled open the sliding door and hopped in.

"Hi, Mrs. Berg," I said.

She smiled at me. "How are you doing, Fish?"

"Good," I said. It was kind of a lie. I wasn't good. I was nervous and filled with dread. Nervous because in a minute I'd be sharing a seat with my former best friend turned enemy. And dread because I was going to have to tell the rabbi I would be doing my bar mitzvah project with that enemy. Collecting smelly old hockey equipment. With a kid who hated my guts.

Seth's mom looked at the back door of the school. "I thought Seth would be with you."

"He was talking to Mandy at his locker," I said.

"Oh?" She was smirking. "A girl?"

I nodded. "A friend, I guess."

"Like a girl friend or a *girlfriend*?"

Good question. One I didn't know the answer to. Seth had never said he was interested in Mandy like *that*. He'd never mentioned her at all. I could see why he might be though—she was nice. Definitely nicer than him. Especially right now.

"I don't know." I looked out the side window. "Oh, there he is."

Thankfully. This conversation was getting awkward.

Seth pulled open the sliding door and got in beside me. He didn't even look at me.

"Hi, Mom," he said and then started talking about his project, reminding her that she had promised to drive him to the Westside arena on Sunday to pick up all the donated equipment. He was talking like I wasn't even there.

Well, I *was* there. "What time?" I said, interrupting. "I'll come to your house, and we can go together."

Seth slowly turned his head and looked at me. He was not smiling. "Go *together*? What are you talking about?"

I cleared my throat. "For the project. Since I'm doing it with you."

He frowned. "No, you're not. Braden's doing it with me."

"But..." I suddenly had to blink away tears. "You told your coach I was doing it with you."

He shook his head. "No, I didn't. Why would I do that? You don't even like hockey. Braden's doing it."

"Seth," his mom said. "There must be room for another helper."

"There isn't," he said.

"It's okay, Mrs. Berg," I said, my voice wavering. I did not want to cry. But my best friend was making it very hard not to. "I—I'll find something else to do."

Somehow. And in the next half hour. I didn't say that part.

"I can talk to the coach," said Mrs. Berg. She started the car and pulled away from the school. "I'm sure he'd be okay with you joining in, Fishel."

Seth glared at me. He was telling me with his eyes that I'd better not let his mom talk to the coach for me.

Like I even wanted her to. Still, it hurt that he was so mad at me. He wasn't just mad. It was like he really hated me now. What had I done? This was all over knitting? Seriously?

I cleared my thick throat. "No," I said, trying to smile at her. "It's all right, Mrs. Berg. Hockey isn't my favorite thing anyway."

Understatement of the century.

Chapter Ten

"Fishel, you have to pick *something*," Rabbi Seigel said in a disappointed voice. He was going around to all of us in the bar and bat mitzvah class to find out how our mitzvah projects were coming along.

Then he got to me. I just stared at him. Everyone else had things to report. I had...nothing.

"I had an idea, but it's not going to work out," I explained, looking down at the table. I hated disappointing him. He was a really cool rabbi, even though he'd only been at our synagogue for a year. And while Bubby complained that he seemed too young, I knew she really liked him. We all did.

"And what was that?" Rabbi asked. "Maybe we can figure it out together."

Seth snorted and then covered it up with a cough.

I ignored Seth. Or tried to. I shook my head. "No, Rabbi, it's—it just won't work. Can I please have until next week? I'll figure something out. I promise."

"I'm afraid not, Fish. I'm sorry." He only sounded sort of sorry. "Everyone had plenty of time. I understand it's a big decision, but you should have made it by now."

"So…" I swallowed back tears. "Are you kicking me out of bar mitzvah class?"

I hoped not. My mom would freak out.

Rabbi smiled and shook his head. "Nothing that drastic. And I still want you to do something meaningful. I can't have you dithering about it for weeks though."

"What does that mean?"

"You can do your project at Shalom Village. They are desperate for volunteers."

Shalom Village? That was the retirement home next door to the JCC.

"What you do for them is up to you—I'm not going to decide for you. But now you know where you're doing it. Tracey is the volunteer coordinator there. I'm sure she can help you figure out what to do."

"Oh. Okay," I said. Because what else could I say? "I'll get my mom to take me there on Sunday."

Rabbi nodded. "Good. I'll let Tracey know you're coming. I will expect to hear about the focus of your mitzvah project by next Thursday."

I heard a snicker and looked over at Seth. He was looking at me like, Ha ha, sucker!

Whatever. I glared back at him. Maybe I didn't know what I was going to do at the seniors' home.

But whatever it was, it was going to be way better than collecting hockey equipment.

At the end of our class, Seth rushed out. I grabbed my backpack and got ready to follow, but Rabbi said my name.

Ugh. What now?

"Do you have a minute?" he asked.

"Actually, Seth's mom is waiting."

"It'll just take a second."

"Okay."

He gave me a concerned look. "Fishel, I just wanted to make sure you're all right."

I shrugged. "I'm fine."

"Do you want to tell me about the project you planned that didn't work out?"

"Not really."

Rabbi smiled. "Come on, Fish. I'd like to hear it. I'm always trying to come up with fresh ideas to suggest to kids. I'm sure yours was good. Maybe it just needed some tweaking."

"It was stupid," I said, not looking at him.

"I'm sure it wasn't."

I sighed. "Fine." So I told him.

"Fish," he said, "that's a great idea. Very inspiring. I'm sorry you're not going to be able to make it happen in time for it to be your project. But," he added, pausing until I looked up at him, "mitzvah projects are supposed to get you thinking and encourage you to live a good life filled with mitzvot. To always be thinking of others."

"Okay," I said, not sure what he was getting at.

"I still think you should try to do it." He looked like he really thought it was a good idea.

"You don't think it's stupid that I want to knit?"

"I don't think it's stupid at all," he said. "If it's something you want to do, something you have a passion for, it's the most authentic way for you to give of yourself."

There was that word again. *Passion*.

"You don't think it's too girly?"

"What?" He frowned. "Girly?"

I suddenly regretted asking. "Never mind."

"Fishel," he said. "I don't think people should label activities that way. It's wrong to say some things are for boys or girls."

"That's what *I* thought!" I said. "It doesn't make sense that I can't do something because I'm a boy."

"No, it doesn't," he agreed. "And someone accusing you of doing something *girly* or *feminine* or calling you a girl isn't just an insult to you. It's an insult to girls and women. That kind of language—making *girly* a bad thing or making feminine things something less—hurts everyone. Do you understand that?"

"I think so," I said. But I was still confused. "I mean…sort of?"

"Words like that create hurtful stereotypes. Ideas of women—and men—that are unrealistic and harmful. Even things like petty insults can have a much bigger impact than people realize."

Maybe *that* should be a mitzvah project, I thought. Teaching people about stereotypes and how hurtful they can be.

"Is this why you and Seth aren't talking?" Rabbi asked.

"I..." I suddenly wanted to tell him everything. I wanted to ask him how to fix my friendship. How to make Seth understand.

But what would I say? Could I do it in two minutes? And could I do it without crying? Probably not.

No, definitely not.

Just then I got a text. It was Seth, telling me they were going to leave without me if I didn't hurry up. I doubted his mom would do that, but the text saved me from this very awkward conversation.

I cleared my throat. "Sorry, Rabbi. I have to go. My ride is waiting."

And then I ran out.

Chapter Eleven

Friday morning meant another bus ride sitting up front with Karla's purse.

I was really starting to hate that purse.

After morning classes I took my lunch to the library. The good part of not eating with Seth and the others was I could bring egg salad. Egg salad was my favorite. But Steven always said the smell of eggs made him want to barf, so I'd never had it at school until now.

In the library by myself, no one complained about my lunch.

While I ate, I studied the knitting book again. I was excited to go back to Knitting Club on Monday. I just wished I had needles to practice with over the weekend.

If only my bubby had been willing to teach me. I was still sad about that. Especially when I thought about what Rabbi had said. How activities weren't supposed to be just for boys or just for girls. How they were for whoever wanted to do them.

Why didn't Bubby know that? It didn't make sense. Rabbi had explained how saying that something was only for girls was an insult to girls and women, and I understood that now. But my grandmother was a woman. So how did that work? It was confusing.

I'd thought maybe she wanted to keep knitting a secret from me. Like it was a club that boys weren't allowed in.

But Ms. Harper had said her knitting club was open to everyone. She'd said we shouldn't let people tell us what we can and can't do.

Could my bubby have it wrong? Did she think less of me because I wanted to knit?

It hurt my brain to think about it.

So instead I focused on my book. And my really delicious egg-salad sandwich.

"How was your bar mitzvah class last night?" Mom asked at Shabbat dinner. She'd been out at her book club the night before, and I was asleep when she came home.

I said it was fine. I didn't want to tell her what a jerk Seth had been. Then I remembered my project.

"Oh, and I'll be doing my mitzvah project at Shalom Village—the retirement home next door to the JCC. Can one of you take me there on Sunday morning before my visit with Bubby and Zaida? I have to meet with the volunteer lady there."

I looked at her and then at Darren. Darren had a weird look on his face. Maybe he'd had a bad day at work.

"Sure," Mom said. "I can take you. What are you going to do there?"

"Something with the old people." I shrugged. "Whatever they need me for, I guess."

I loaded some mashed potatoes onto my fork.

Norah made a gurgling noise. I looked up and saw she was squashing her hands together, mashed potatoes oozing out between her fingers. The giant grin on her face said it all—she was loving it.

"Norah! That's gross," I said with a laugh.

She laughed too, then started eating the potatoes off her fingers. Even more gross.

Mom just shook her head.

"So, Fishel," Darren said. His voice seemed very serious and stern.

I looked at him. "Yeah?"

"Is there something you want to tell us?" he asked.

My heart began to race. I glanced at Mom. She shrugged.

"About what?" I said, trying to stay calm. I had a feeling I was in trouble. But for what?

"Why don't you tell me?" Darren said.

That could mean anything. Was it about my fight with Seth? Or taking knitting classes? Or...maybe... ugh! It could be anything!

He'd caught me this way before—by faking me out. I'd ended up getting grounded for something he hadn't even known about. Not again!

Best to pretend I had no idea what he was talking about. "I'm looking forward to the new season of *Dancing with the Stars*, if that's what you mean."

He frowned. "That's not what I mean, young

man, and you know it."

"Darren," Mom said. "What's going on?"

Darren sighed. "I ran into Tom Sherman at the coffee shop today. He told me he's coaching water polo at the JCC this year."

Uh-oh.

I forked a giant glob of potatoes into my mouth.

"Oh," Mom said, smiling. "So he's coaching you, Fish. How great!"

"It would be," Darren said. "If Fish had actually shown up."

Mom's smile disappeared. "What? He was there— we went to the JCC together!"

Gulp. I shoveled even more potatoes into my mouth. I felt like a chipmunk preparing for winter, my cheeks were so full!

"Tom said you weren't in the pool on Wednesday."

I was still chewing the potatoes, staring down at my plate. My gut said I should deny it. But there was no way of getting out of this. Darren *knew* I hadn't been there. He was already mad. He'd be off-the-charts mad if I lied about it.

I finished chewing. Swallowed. Took a sip from my water glass. Then I took a deep breath and finally looked up at him. "I didn't go."

"Obviously," Darren said. "What I want to know is why."

"Because I really, really, *really* didn't want to go to water polo."

"Why didn't you just say so?" Mom asked.

My throat suddenly got dry and sore like the last time I'd had a cold. I took another sip of water and swallowed hard. "I tried to. You wouldn't listen."

"So you just skipped it," Darren said. "And wasted all that money."

"No!" I shook my head. "I didn't waste the money. I changed to Zum—something else."

"What do you mean?" Mom asked, looking confused. "There wasn't anything else."

I swallowed. "I...uh...I switched to the Zumba class."

There was a big silence. Norah filled it with a raspberry that sprayed potatoes everywhere. I had to press my lips together so I wouldn't laugh. My little sister had the best timing. Or maybe the worst timing. Neither Mom nor Darren looked amused.

"Wait," Mom said, looking at me sideways. "You took the *seniors'* Zumba class?"

I nodded.

"You dropped out of water polo to take seniors' Zumba?" Darren looked really mad now.

I nodded again.

"And then you lied about it."

It wasn't a question. But he seemed to want an answer anyway. I nodded again as my eyes filled with tears. I tried to make them go away, but it didn't work. You can't wish tears away.

Darren shook his head and stabbed at his steak with his fork. "Well, you're going to switch back to water polo."

"No," I said. "I'm not."

"What?" Darren demanded.

I looked at my mom. She wasn't saying anything.

I thought about Ms. Harper and how strong she'd been about not getting pressured into doing things she didn't want to do. I took another deep breath. "I'm not going back to water polo. I liked Zumba, and that's what I want to do."

Darren snorted. "Seniors' Zumba. That's what you want to do."

"Yes!" I said, mad now. "That's what I want to do. They didn't mind, so why do you?!"

Darren rolled his eyes. "And now you're crying." He said it in the same tone of voice Seth had used when he found out about the knitting.

Which made me cry even more.

I dropped my head, tears falling into my mashed potatoes. Darren didn't understand. He didn't understand anything.

"Fishel!" Darren barked. "Why are you crying?"

Norah squeaked. Then *she* started crying.

"Darren!" Mom said. She wasn't yelling, but her tone was really stern. "There is no need to raise your voice!"

Darren huffed. "Stop that crying right now, Fishel. Boys don't cry."

I looked up at him, the tears rolling down my face now. "Yes they do. I saw lots of boys—and grown-up men—crying at my dad's funeral."

Mom gasped. "Fishel..."

But I wasn't done. "No one said *that* was wrong, so why is it wrong to be upset now? I'm a boy, and I'm crying. So boys *do* cry. And if they want to, they can do things like knitting and going to Zumba. None of those things make me less of a boy!"

Norah wailed. Mom and Darren stared at me, neither of them saying a word.

I pushed my chair back and ran out of the kitchen.

Chapter Twelve

I threw myself down on my bed and cried so hard that I gave myself the hiccups. Eventually I stopped crying. The hiccups didn't stop though.

Through the door I heard Norah finally stop crying too. I felt bad for upsetting her, but I couldn't help it. It was more Darren's fault anyway. I hoped he was sorry.

There was a knock on my door. I wiped my face with the sleeve of my shirt. Then I took a deep breath, hiccupped and answered, "What?"

"It's Mom. Can I please come in, Fishel?"

I sighed. "Fine."

I had to wipe my face again because the tears had returned. Mom came in, closing the door behind her. She sat on my bed.

I hiccupped.

"You okay?" she asked. It was a silly question.

"No."

She reached out and gave my arm a squeeze. "Want to tell me what's going on?"

"Not really."

She smiled. "Fish, come on. Remember when it was just you and me? Before Darren and Norah came along? We told each other everything, didn't we?"

I shrugged. "That was before you, Bubby and Darren decided what I could and couldn't do."

"Bubby?" She frowned. "Wait. What?"

"Never mind."

Mom squeezed my arm again. "No, Fishel, tell me. I want to understand what's going on here."

She looked sad. But also like she wanted to help.

So I told her everything. From the idea I'd gotten for my bar mitzvah project to how Bubby had said boys didn't knit, even how Seth had made fun of me. I also told her what Ms. Harper and Rabbi Seigel had said.

She listened to it all, paying close attention. She let me talk without interrupting me until I was done.

By the end of it, my hiccups were gone. So were my tears. But Mom looked like maybe she had some in her eyes.

"Fishel," she said. And then, without warning, she pulled me into her arms for a big hug. She squeezed me so tight I felt crushed. And pretty loved. But mostly crushed.

"Mom," I grunted. "I can't breathe!"

"I'm sorry, Fish." She let me go. "I just...I'm so sorry about all of this. Both the rabbi and your knitting teacher are right. They are 100 percent right. You should do whatever you are passionate about— whatever that is."

"Darren and Bubby don't think so. Neither do Seth, Steven and Amir."

She sighed. "Well, they're wrong. I don't like that you lied about the water polo, but I understand you felt like you didn't have a choice. Forcing that on you wasn't fair. We need to do better."

"Mom, I *really* don't like sports."

She nodded. "If I'd taken a moment to think about it, I would have realized it wasn't your thing. Even though Darren was so sure of it. I listened to him when I should have known better. I'm so sorry, Fish. I want you to try new things, and I got caught up in it all."

"I did try something new," I reminded her. "Zumba. I loved it."

"It *is* fun, isn't it?" She smiled and booped my nose. "I bet you were good at it too."

I nodded. "The teacher said he wouldn't have known it was my first time."

"I'm not surprised." Mom paused for a moment. "And about the knitting thing..."

I suddenly got scared she was going to tell me I couldn't be in Knitting Club. I took a breath and held it.

"Your mitzvah project sounds wonderful. I want to support you in any way I can. Tell me how I can help."

"It's too late," I said.

She lifted an eyebrow. "Oh, I don't know. I think if there's a will, there's a way."

"What do you mean?" I asked. My heart started pounding in excitement. She thought it was a great idea. And it seemed like she was saying maybe there was a way we could still do it.

"I mean that if we put our heads together, we can make anything happen. You have until next Thursday, right?"

I shook my head. "Rabbi Seigel said I have to do my project at Shalom Village. He said I didn't have enough time to do the knitting project."

Mom wiggled both her eyebrows. "Well then, it's a good thing that Shalom Village factors into my idea."

Then she told me *her* plan.

It was perfect. Better than my original plan by 1,000 percent.

I threw myself into my mom's arms. "Thank you, Mom," I said. "Thank you so much."

When our hug was done, she looked into my eyes. "Fish, do you forgive me for trying to force you to do something you didn't want to do?"

"That depends," I said, pretending to be more upset than I was.

"Cheeky!" she said, laughing. "What does it depend on?"

"Will you take me to the yarn store?"

She stood up. "Go wash your face, and I'll get my keys. They're open until nine."

"But it's Shabbat!" I said, jumping up off the bed. "We never go out on Friday nights."

"Oh, I think we can make an exception this once. I know how important this is to you, Fish."

That's when I knew she was just as excited as I was.

And that my mitzvah project was going to be amazing.

Chapter Thirteen

On Sunday morning the four of us—Norah, Mom, Darren and me—went for brunch. I was super excited, and not just about brunch. Afterward Mom and I were going to go to Shalom Village to talk to the volunteer lady, Tracey, about my project.

We took two cars so that after we'd eaten, Norah could go home with Darren. I was still a bit mad at him, but Mom must have given him a talking to, because he'd apologized and said I could do whatever activity I wanted. I could tell he still didn't like that I had picked Zumba over water polo, but Mom had whispered to me that I should just ignore it and accept his apology. So I had.

At brunch I had my favorite meal in the world (not including ice cream). A waffle with sliced strawberries, custard and whipped cream. It was so huge I didn't even mind sharing it with Norah. She really didn't eat much anyway. More ended up outside her mouth than in it.

When Mom and I got to Shalom Village, I felt jittery with excitement. We left the shopping bags full of stuff in the car and went inside to the main office.

There was an older lady at the front counter. She was wearing a badge that said *EDNA—Volunteer*. I wondered if she lived upstairs in one of the seniors' apartments.

She looked up and smiled. "Can I help you?"

"Hi!" I said. "We're here to see Tracey?"

"Sure," she said. She looked over at an open doorway to an office. I couldn't see inside but could hear voices. There was a sign beside the door that said *Tracey Billings—Volunteer Coordinator*.

"She's in a meeting right now. Is she expecting you?" Edna asked.

"Yes." Mom put her hand on my shoulder. "We were just hoping to talk to her about my son's bar mitzvah project."

Edna stood up. "I'm sure I can interrupt." She smiled at me. "What's your name?"

"Fish—I mean, Fishel Rosner," I said.

A man's voice boomed out. "I thought I heard you, Fish!"

I looked up and there was the rabbi, coming out of the office. A woman was beside him.

"How's that for timing?" Rabbi Seigel said. He turned to the woman. "Tracey, this is Fishel Rosner, the boy I was telling you about. I assume he and his mom, Judy, are here to talk to you about his mitzvah project."

"Yes," I said. I shifted from one foot to the other and back. I was seriously so excited.

"Well, I'll leave you to it," Rabbi Seigel said. "I've got my Torah study shortly. Nice to see you, Judy. See you Thursday, Fish."

"Rabbi!" I blurted out. "Maybe…can you stay? Please?"

He looked from me to Tracey and back to me again.

"I think you'll want to hear this, Rabbi," Mom said.

"Well," Tracey said. "I have to say I'm intrigued!"

She waved the four of us into her office, and we all sat down. Mom and I—but mostly me—explained what we wanted to do.

They loved it. In fact, by the time Mom and I went out to the car to get the yarn and other supplies, Rabbi and Tracey were as excited as we were. So excited that

Tracey asked if we could stay until lunchtime, when she'd make an announcement in the dining hall.

Of course we did.

At the end of her announcement, which made my project sound even cooler and more exciting, there was a huge round of applause and lots of people started talking. As Tracey sent around a sheet for sign-ups, the seniors were almost fighting over who got to sign up first.

Mom looked happy. And really, really proud.

We were finally leaving Shalom Village. It was way later than we'd expected, but that was okay. We'd been doing important things. We'd texted Bubby to say I'd be a bit late for my visit. She didn't mind.

We were headed for the parking lot when I heard my name. I turned around. At first it seemed weird to see a young man in shorts and bright blue sneakers standing in a seniors' home. Then it all clicked.

It was Richard, the dance instructor. "Here for more Zumba?" he asked.

"Ha!" I grinned back at him. "Actually, if it's okay, I'd still like to come to class."

Richard looked at my mother.

Mom nodded. "He's welcome to, if you don't mind that he's a bit younger than the rest of the class."

Richard laughed. "Works for me. It was great to have you, Fish. The others thought so too."

"Awesome," I said. "See you Wednesday."

He gave me a fist bump.

Seriously, could this day get any better?

Most Sundays Mom dropped me off at the front doors of the condo building. Not today. She said she wanted to talk to my grandparents.

"Is that a bad thing or a good thing?" I asked.

"A good thing," Mom said, but her tone made me think it was a little bad. She parked in a spot with a big V on it—for visitors—and went with me into the building. I pressed the elevator button, and we rode up to the eleventh floor. With every floor, I got a little more nervous. She seemed nervous too. Which made me even more nervous.

When we got to apartment D, I knocked. "It's me, Fishel. And Mom," I added.

Bubby opened the door and smiled at my mom. "Judy, how nice to see you." She seemed to mean it, but she looked confused too.

"Sorry we're late," Mom said. She bent over to give my grandmother a kiss on the cheek. "I was hoping the four of us could chat."

"Of course," Bubby said. Then she turned toward the den and hollered, "Jeffrey, can you turn off the TV and come out here for a minute?"

"It's the last inning!" Zaida yelled back.

We all laughed. He sure loved sports. Bubby rolled her eyes. "Put the PVR on! That's why we got it!"

She led us into the living room, and we sat down. A minute later Zaida arrived. "Oh, hello, Judy. Hi, Fish."

Mom got up and greeted Zaida with a kiss on the cheek before sitting down again. "I just want to talk to you for a few minutes."

Zaida and Bubby exchanged looks.

Bubby turned to Mom. "Is this a 'few minutes' conversation or an 'I should put on a pot of coffee' conversation?"

Mom thought about that for a minute.

"Let me save you some trouble," Bubby said. "If this is about Fish's mitzvah project, I already know about it. My friend Maggie Cohen was so excited about it that she called me twenty minutes ago."

Maggie Cohen—the lady from Zumba—must have been at Shalom Village for the big announcement.

"Oh," Mom said. "That's great."

"It's a wonderful idea, Fish," Bubby said. "Of course, I'm happy to be one of your knitters."

I nodded. Then I cleared my throat. "Thanks. But...I'm going to knit too."

Bubby pressed her lips together.

"Because boys can knit," I said, trying to make my voice strong.

"Of course they can," Zaida said, frowning.

"Jeffrey," Bubby said.

Zaida looked at her. "What's wrong? Are you saying boys can't knit?"

"Of course they can. But...I just worry..." Her eyes darted toward me, and then she said softly, "Other kids will make fun."

She was trying to protect me. Too late for that. "Bubby, other kids have already made fun of me for it. But I don't care. I want to knit, and I am *going to* knit. I've even joined the knitting club at school."

"Why do you need to join a club?" Bubby asked with a frown.

I swallowed hard. "Because you wouldn't teach me."

Bubby's face got all red. Not mad red, but embarrassed red. She looked down at her hands in her lap.

"Is that true?" Zaida asked her.

Bubby didn't look up, but she nodded.

"I asked her last week when I was here," I said. "She told me to watch sports with you instead."

"*Told* you to watch sports?" Zaida asked. "I thought you *liked* watching sports with me."

I shrugged. "I like hanging out with you, but not the sports. I actually don't like sports at all."

He stared at me for a long minute. "Your grandmother won't teach you to knit, and I make you watch sports you don't like. Your visits here must be pretty awful."

I cringed. "I wouldn't use the word *awful*."

One of Zaida's bushy eyebrows went up. Mom snorted.

"How about there's room for improvement?" I said.

Zaida twisted his mouth into a frown. "That is…

very kind." Then he made a noise that was something between a snort and a laugh. He turned to Bubby. "Sandy, if the boy wants to learn to knit, you should teach him how to knit."

Bubby nodded. "Yes. I...I'm sorry, Fishel. I...I guess I wasn't thinking."

"And maybe I'll watch," Zaida said.

"You?" Bubby said, shocked. "Watch knitting? Since when are you interested in knitting?"

Zaida shrugged. "I've always been impressed by what you create. Your socks are works of art, magical. I wish I could make them too."

"Really?" Bubby said, and I could tell she'd never heard this from Zaida before. It seemed weird—they'd been married forever.

Zaida held up his big hands. "I don't think I could, with my fat sausage fingers."

Bubby blinked a few times. "Well, if you want to learn, I think we could work around your big fingers. I could teach the two of you together."

I grinned at my grandfather.

He winked and grinned back.

I looked over at my grandmother. "And you'll help with my project?"

She smiled at me proudly. "You couldn't stop me, Fishel."

"Well," Mom said. She stood up. "I guess that's that. I'll go down to the car and be right back. Come and help me, Fish."

"Help with what?" Bubby asked.

Mom's smile was really wide. "You didn't think we'd enlist your help and not bring over supplies, did you?"

Bubby laughed. "Oh dear. What have I agreed to?" She didn't really mean it, I could tell. In fact, she gave me a big hug and whispered in my ear how sorry she was. And then she said, "I'm so proud of you, Fishel."

Chapter Fourteen

By Monday afternoon I'd had enough of sitting at the front of the bus.

I did not want to spend even one more bus ride next to Karla's purse.

I was tired of how Seth was treating me. I didn't want to be ignored anymore. I couldn't pretend we'd never been friends anymore. I didn't want to not *be* friends anymore.

I had to gather up all my courage and fix things.

"Seth," I said when we got to our lockers after last period. It was noisy in the hall, but I didn't care. I was so over this fight. "Can we please make up?"

He stared at me for a long time. Then he smirked. "Make up? Now you want to wear makeup?"

I huffed. "Seth, don't be such a jerk! You know what I meant. I want to end this stupid fight."

He tilted his head like he didn't understand. "I didn't know we were fighting. I thought you wanted to hang out with the girls and knit and go to tea parties."

He must have forgotten how *he* had been the one to run away from *me*. Whatever. I was starting to wonder why I had ever wanted to be his friend in the first place. "Why are you acting like this? Why do you care what I do so much?"

"Oh, look at *Miss* Rosner getting all upset." He turned toward Steven, who had just walked over. "Girls can get *so* emotional."

Steven laughed.

I narrowed my eyes at Seth. My heart was pounding hard. I wanted to push him down, but I had to fight back with my words or he would never understand.

I took a deep breath. "You know, when you say stuff like that, it's not just stupid—it's insulting to your mom and your sister."

He frowned. "My mom and my sister?" He looked around. "They aren't here."

"No, but telling someone he acts like a girl and meaning it as an insult is insulting to all girls."

He sneered at me. "It's an insult to you."

For some reason his words didn't bother me this time. It wasn't an insult if I didn't get insulted. But even so, I had to stand up to him. His words were still hurtful. Just not to me.

I crossed my arms. "What's so bad about being a girl? Because that's what you're really saying. That it would be bad if I was a girl. Like girls aren't as good as boys."

I felt a nudge on my shoulder. I turned to see Mandy standing next to me. She gave me a nod. Then she looked at Seth. "Yeah, Seth. Why *is* it bad to be a girl? Are you saying boys are better than girls?"

Seth's smile faltered. He looked from me to Mandy. Then his smile completely disappeared. "I didn't say it was bad to be a girl," he said quietly, head down.

"Yes, you did," Mandy said. "When you called Fish *Miss* as an insult." She rolled her eyes. "Even though it was a stupid insult. Like being a *Miss* is a bad thing."

"Which it's not," I said.

Mandy smiled at me. "Exactly. The only bad thing about being a Miss is that we have to put up with jerks like Seth."

"And his stupid insults," I added.

Seth was obviously shocked. He started to stutter, then clamped his mouth shut. He didn't even have a good comeback.

Steven laughed.

"And other jerks who follow along. Like you," Mandy added, glaring at Steven. "How unoriginal."

That shut Steven up too.

"Anyway," Mandy said, looping her arm through mine, "I think knitting and tea parties sound like fun, don't you, Fish?"

"So much fun," I said, smiling at Mandy.

Together we turned and walked away from Seth and Steven.

That afternoon I said goodbye to Karla's purse for good. I sat in a seat on the right side of the bus, four rows back, sandwiched between Mandy and Barbie.

We got out our knitting projects, but it was too bumpy on the bus. Barbie said one of us could get jabbed in the eye with a knitting needle if Karla hit a pothole in the road. We put our needles and yarn away. But it was okay. We talked about knitting and what we'd learned at lunch in Knitting Club. We talked about how excited we were to practice and learn more stuff next week.

It felt good. They weren't making fun of me for wanting to knit. I was being myself. And they liked me anyway. Or maybe they liked me *because* I was myself.

Too bad my old friends couldn't. But that was their loss.

When it was Seth's stop, I glanced up as he walked by. He looked at me at the same time.

He wasn't smirking. Or even smiling. He seemed... sad. Maybe even a little guilty.

It was noisy on the bus, but I saw his mouth say the word *sorry*.

Maybe there was still hope for us after all.

Epilogue

Six months later...

I sat on the big throne behind the podium. Normally only the rabbi or the synagogue president got to sit in the big carved wooden chairs at the back of the stage, but today I got the honor. I'd always wondered what it would feel like. Now I knew that the red velvet cushion was lumpy. But it didn't matter—it was my special day.

I was nervous and excited and very relieved. Relieved because it was my bar mitzvah and I'd already finished reading the Torah in Hebrew. And I'd nailed it. Nervous and excited because my English speech—the one I'd had to write myself—was coming up next.

First the rabbi had to finish speaking. He was going on and on about the meaning of my Torah portion and what we should take from it. I already knew all that stuff, so I sort of tuned out. Like I used to when I watched sports with Zaida. Which I didn't do anymore. He never put sports on when I visited now. We did knitting or sometimes we went out— to the yarn store or for nature walks or to the mall. Sometimes just for ice cream, which was okay by me.

I looked out at the audience. There he was with Bubby, in the front row. Our eyes locked, and he winked and smiled at me, also giving me a thumbs-up. I gave him one back.

My eyes scanned the crowd. In the fourth row were all my friends. The kids from Knitting Club were sitting together and whispering to one another, ignoring the rabbi. I didn't mind, since I was ignoring him too. I wondered if they were talking about the new pattern we were working on. At the end of the row was Ms. Harper, wearing her dress with math equations all over it. It was in honor of Hedy Lamarr, the Jewish film star and inventor.

Ms. Harper leaned over to the girls and held her finger to her lips, telling them to hush.

Then she smiled up at me. She looked proud. I smiled back.

Movement caught my eye in the row behind her. It was Seth, adjusting the kippah on his head. Amir and Steven were sitting next to him. Yes, I'd made up with them. Seth had apologized, and I'd explained to him and my other friends how activities were for whoever wanted to do them. And how that was okay. They seemed to understand and promised not to use hurtful words anymore. I'd known they really got it when Amir asked if he could join Knitting Club too. Of course, we had let him.

"...and now a few words about our bar mitzvah, Fishel," Rabbi Seigel said.

I sat up straight.

"Fishel did a wonderful job with his reading this morning. But you may not know how hard he struggled with his mitzvah project in the beginning." He turned and gave me a quick smile before he looked back at the audience.

"He wanted to find something meaningful to him. Something he felt strongly about and could give of himself—something uniquely Fishel.

When he did stumble on his idea, which I'll let him tell you about in a minute, he thought it was too late to make it work. But then he and his mom did a little brainstorming, and they came up with what is now known as Fish's Stitches, a wonderful organization that is touching every part of our community and bringing people together in amazing ways."

He turned toward me, his smile so big and proud I could hardly stand it. "But why don't I let him tell you all about it. Fish?"

I stood up and had to take a big breath. I was really nervous. But I was also so excited I was ready to burst. I couldn't wait to tell everyone all about Fish's Stitches. Most of the people knew part of the story, but I had some big news.

"Hi, everyone," I said once I got to the podium. "Um, thanks for coming."

I read from my notes, thanking the rabbi and my family and saying all the other stuff Mom had told me I needed to say. Then I got to the best part.

"And thank you to everyone who helped with Fish's Stitches. I got the idea when I saw my grandmother—my bubby—making her famous socks. I thought about how much I loved her socks, and how when I wore them it felt like I was getting a hug from her even if she wasn't around."

I glanced down at her in the audience. She was dabbing at her eyes with a tissue. But she was also smiling her big smile, so I knew she liked my speech so far.

"And I thought about how some kids weren't able to have that feeling. Some kids don't have grandparents or even parents. Some kids don't have a home or warm socks knitted for them by someone who cares.

"That's when I decided to care. I decided that I wanted to make socks for every single kid who needs them."

I heard an "aww" from the crowd.

I smiled and continued with my speech. "There was only one problem. I didn't know how to knit!"

The audience laughed.

"I had *no idea* how hard socks are to make!"

More laughs.

"But I got help from my mom," I said, smiling down at her. "And I also got help from my bubby, her friends and lots of the people at Shalom Village who love to knit. The next thing I knew, I had a dozen pairs of socks. It was my job to give them out to kids who needed them. I went to some shelters and residences—wherever there were kids who might need socks."

The room burst into applause. Then people in the audience started getting up. People were moving around and talking.

What was happening? I wasn't finished my speech!

"Wait! I'm not done!" Why wasn't anyone staying in their seats? I started to panic. My throat got tight. Tears filled my eyes. I hadn't even had a chance to tell everyone about the TV crew that was going to interview me about Fish's Stitches!

But then Ms. Harper was in front of me with a giant plastic bin in her arms. She was smiling from ear to ear.

"What's going on?" I whispered.

She slid the bin onto the stage beside me. Then I noticed the lineup of people behind her.

And every single person in that line was holding a pair of socks. Handmade knitted socks. They came up and started piling them into the bin.

Ms. Harper stood beside me at the podium as more and more socks appeared. "Fish, I hope you'll forgive us for keeping this a secret, but when I heard about your project, I thought a few more people would want to help." She laughed. "Turns out I was wrong. A *lot* more people wanted to help."

"Whoa," was all I could say.

She smiled and pointed at the bin. "My own knitting club has been working hard. There are two hundred and fifty-two pairs of socks in there for you to distribute."

"What?" My mouth fell open.

There was a huge roar of applause.

"And your knitting club has been working secretly too."

Mandy, Gail, Ginny, Barbie and Amir came up and put socks in the bin. There were so many pairs now, they were falling onto the stage.

Mrs. Cohen came up. And more people from Shalom Village and my Zumba class. Soon there were so many pairs of socks, I couldn't imagine how we were even going to get them home.

The last two people in line were my grandparents. Bubby held up her own bin, filled with tons of socks. Zaida didn't have a bin. But he was holding up a single pair of socks—one sock in each hand.

I laughed because they looked awful. One was quite a bit bigger than the other, and the smaller one barely even looked like a sock at all. But they were made in my favorite colors, purple, pink and green.

"You made those for the project?" I said. The words almost stuck in my throat. I was so proud of him and everyone who had helped. "With your big sausage fingers!"

"I made them for you," he said with the biggest smile ever. "With my big sausage fingers. Because boys can knit."

When he hugged me super hard, we both had tears in our eyes.

Which is okay. Boys cry when they're really happy too.

Acknowledgments

Most books are hard to write. But once in a while the stars align, the muses cooperate and a book seems to write itself. That's how *Fish Out of Water* came together for me. I'm grateful for the experience, though I suspect it won't happen again. Ever. Ah well, this one time was really nice.

Still, I don't create books in a vacuum, so as always, there are people to thank.

To the people at Orca Book Publishers who made this book possible, starting with Andrew: Your support of Canadian writers and their work is extraordinary and appreciated by all the authors you publish. Big thanks to Ruth, Leslie, Olivia, Kennedy and everyone else who works behind the scenes to get books out there—you're the best. Thank you for all your tireless work.

And Tanya, editor extraordinaire who gets me (and Fish): You are a dream to work with and I'm grateful for your insight and perspective. Here's to many more. I will ever toast you with my Scotch (egg), Karla's giant purse and my felting needles.

To my beta reader for this project, Lisa Dalrymple—thank you for your insight and fresh eyes. You were right in all things!

Thank you also to my agent, Hilary McMahon, a steadfast advocate for her writers who also happens to be one of the loveliest people I've met on this long publishing journey.

As always, my biggest thanks go to my husband, Deke, Team Snow co-captain and unquestioning supporter of me and absolutely everything I do. I mean it, everything I do, even the weird stuff. Maybe especially the weird stuff.

Excerpt

I changed out of that uncomfortable dress, had some lunch and went out to my garden. I kept an eye on the Patels' backyard. Maybe I was hoping to see Jazzy.

No, I was *definitely* hoping to see Jazzy. Since we were going to be best friends and all. May as well get started on that, I figured.

But she didn't come out of the house. I didn't want to interrupt whatever she was doing inside, so I focused on picking sugar snap peas. I wondered if Jazzy liked peas. They'd been Anna's favorite, which was why I had planted them in the first place.

Now I saved them for Maisey and Daisy—the cute twins across the street. They liked popping the little peas out of their pods and straight into their mouths. I'd take some over to them later.

Soon I was done the day's harvest—peas, tomatoes and the dreaded broccoli. Jazzy still hadn't come out. I started pulling some weeds.

Still no Jazzy.

Maybe she was watching a movie or helping prepare dinner. I tried not to let my imagination come up with a zillion reasons why she wasn't coming to see me—her soon-to-be new best friend. Except it was all I could think about.

I went into the house and traded the basket of fresh vegetables for the compost bin we keep under the counter. I took it outside.

Still no Jazzy.

I took the compost into the shed and pulled the lid off my worm bin.

Yes, I said worm bin. As in real, live worms. Red wigglers, to be precise. I pulled back the newspaper bedding and dug a hole for the scraps. Banana peels, strawberry tops, chopped-up broccoli stalks.

I knew my worms would eat everything, even the vegetables I didn't like. I fed them our kitchen scraps, and they made organic fertilizer. We have a great relationship that way. Not quite a friendship. But as I thought about the hug I'd received from the Patels' granddaughter, I hoped that now I'd have a *real* friend. With arms and everything.

I looked out the dirty window of the shed.

Finally! There she was! I watched her open the sliding glass door at the back of the house and head toward my yard. She had a big smile on her face. One that matched mine.

I quickly put the rest of the scraps into the bin, covered them up and closed the lid. I stepped out of the shed and called out a loud, "Hi!"

Jazzy looked at me, her smile disappearing. "Oh, hi there." She glanced over toward the house. "I'm looking for Victoria."

"Huh?" I asked. Because, uh, I am Victoria.

"I met her earlier," Jazzy said. "She was wearing a stunning green dress. Elegant hair, sparkly shoes?"

She was looking at me like we'd never met. I was starting to think maybe she was a little nuts.

Then I looked down at myself. Ratty old T-shirt and jeans, hands covered in worm and food-scrap muck. My hair shoved under a baseball cap, and Crocs caked with mud. Hardly elegant.

"Oh, I..."

"Ugh, what is that all over your hands?" Jazzy asked with a frown.

I put my arms behind my back, even though it was too late to hide them. "Worm castings."

Her frown went from disgust to confusion. "What are worm *castings*?"

"Worm poop," I said, though very quietly, like maybe she wouldn't hear.

"WORM POOP?!" Nope, nothing wrong with her hearing. "Like, poop from actual worms?"

I nodded. I was thinking how nice it would have been to have a new best friend. Not much chance of that now.

"Worm. Poop." She gagged. "That is *disgusting*."

"It's not as gross as it sounds," I said a bit helplessly. "It's for my garden." I waved toward my vegetable beds.

"Poop. You put worm poop in your garden."

I was getting annoyed that she kept repeating herself. But what could I do? I just nodded.

"Gross."

I just stood there, silent.

"Anyway," she said, crossing her arms. Her shirt had a big daisy on the front of it. "I'm here to see Vicky. Is she around? We were going to hang out."

So...wait. Jazzy *still* didn't recognize me as the girl she'd met earlier? *And* she was calling *that girl* Vicky?

As Jazzy stared at me like I was simple, I stared at her shirt. It made me think of Daisy across the street.

I suddenly had an idea. One that might save the best-friend thing. "Oh, right," I said quickly. "Vicky is inside having a nap. I'm her twin sister, Tori."

Okay, so I didn't say that it was a *good* idea.

Joanne Levy is the author of a number of books for young people, including *Double Trouble* from the Orca Currents line and the middle-grade novels *Crushing It* and the Red Maple–nominated *Small Medium At Large*. She lives in Clinton, Ontario.

For more information on all the books

in the Orca Currents line, please visit

orcabook.com.